W9-CSL-020

My Secret Unicorn

Keeper of Magic

Lauren looked at the box. What was inside?
As she held it, a tingle of magic seemed to creep
over her fingers. Lauren was sure that whatever
was in the box was something about unicorns.
If only she could open it. But she had to wait.
How long for though? When *would* it be the
right time?

Books in the series

THE MAGIC SPELL

DREAMS COME TRUE

FLYING HIGH

STARLIGHT SURPRISE

STRONGER THAN MAGIC

A SPECIAL FRIEND

A WINTER WISH

A TOUCH OF MAGIC

SNOWY DREAMS

TWILIGHT MAGIC

FRIENDS FOREVER

RISING STAR

MOONLIGHT JOURNEY

KEEPER OF MAGIC

My Secret Unicorn

Keeper of Magic

Linda Chapman

Illustrated by Ann Kronheimer

PUFFIN

PUFFIN BOOKS

Published by the Penguin Group
Penguin Books Ltd, 80 Strand, London WC2R ORL, England
Penguin Group (USA) Inc., 375 Hudson Street, New York, New York 10014, USA
Penguin Group (Canada), 90 Eglinton Avenue East, Suite 700, Toronto, Ontario, Canada M4P 2Y3
(a division of Pearson Penguin Canada Inc.)
Penguin Ireland, 25 St Stephen's Green, Dublin 2, Ireland (a division of Penguin Books Ltd)
Penguin Group (Australia), 250 Camberwell Road, Camberwell, Victoria 3124, Australia
(a division of Pearson Australia Group Pty Ltd)
Penguin Books India Pvt Ltd, 11 Community Centre, Panchsheel Park,
New Delhi – 110 017, India
Penguin Group (NZ), 67 Apollo Drive, Rosedale, North Shore 0632, New Zealand
(a division of Pearson New Zealand Ltd)
Penguin Books (South Africa) (Pty) Ltd, 24 Sturdee Avenue, Rosebank,
Johannesburg 2196, South Africa

Penguin Books Ltd, Registered Offices: 80 Strand, London WC2R ORL, England

penguin.com

Published 2007
1

Text copyright © Working Partners Ltd, 2007
Illustrations copyright © Ann Kronheimer, 2007
All rights reserved

The moral right of the author and illustrator has been asserted

Set in Bembo
Typeset by Palimpsest Book Production Limited, Grangemouth, Stirlingshire
Made and printed in England by Clays Ltd, St Ives plc

Except in the United States of America, this book is sold subject to the condition
that it shall not, by way of trade or otherwise, be lent, re-sold, hired out, or otherwise
circulated without the publisher's prior consent in any form of binding or cover other
than that in which it is published and without a similar condition including this condition
being imposed on the subsequent purchaser

British Library Cataloguing in Publication Data
A CIP catalogue record for this book is available from the British Library

ISBN: 978-0-141-32122-6

*To Helen Levene, my Puffin editor,
for loving Lauren and Twilight as much as
I do and for sharing their adventures with
such skill and enthusiasm. Thank you.*

CHAPTER
One

'Higher, Twilight!' Lauren laughed in delight as Twilight swooped over the treetops. His snowy-white neck was warm beneath her hands and his ears were pricked up. Happiness rushed through Lauren as the stars blurred around them. She felt as if she could go on flying forever. She loved having a unicorn of her own!

'This is fun!' Twilight said as he
swooped down and jumped over the top
branches of an oak tree. His mouth
didn't move but as long as Lauren was
either touching him or holding a hair
from his mane she could hear his voice
in her head as clearly as if he had
spoken. It was part of his unicorn magic.
Most of the time, Twilight looked just
like any other small grey pony, but when
Lauren said the magic words of the
Turning Spell, he changed into a
beautiful unicorn with a glittering
silver horn.

'I wish I could tell Hannah about you,
Twilight,' Lauren said, thinking about her
fourteen-year-old cousin who was

coming to stay in a day's time. Hannah lived a long way away so they didn't get to see each other much but Hannah loved ponies and Lauren got on with her really well. Lauren knew Hannah would have loved to have seen Twilight as a unicorn but unicorn magic had to be kept secret from anyone who didn't have a unicorn of their own.

'I can't wait to meet her,' Twilight said. 'What's she like?'

'Pony crazy,' Lauren answered with a grin. 'Mum has arranged for her to borrow a horse from Orchard Stables while she's here so we'll be able to go on long rides together.' She patted Twilight. She couldn't wait for Hannah to meet him, even if she would only see him when he was a pony. 'We'd better go home now,' she said. 'It's getting late.'

They flew back to Granger's Farm where Lauren lived with her mum, dad, eight-year-old brother, Max, and Buddy, his Bernese mountain dog. Twilight's paddock was tucked away around the back of the farm and could only be seen from Lauren's bedroom window. Behind it towered the shadowy wooded slopes of the Blue Ridge Mountains. Twilight landed lightly on the short winter grass. Lauren dismounted and was immediately aware of the chill of the air on her face. When she was on Twilight's back, his unicorn magic meant that she never felt cold, but now she was on the ground, she could feel the damp in the November air.

'I'll put your rug on you tonight to keep you warm,' she told him.

He nuzzled her. 'Thank you.'

Lauren quickly said the magic words of the Undoing Spell that changed him back into a pony.

There was a flash and suddenly Twilight was standing there looking just like any other regular grey pony. His winter coat was long and fluffy and his mane and tail were slightly tangled but there was still a magical sparkle in his eyes.

Lauren fetched his waterproof New Zealand rug from the tack room and quickly rugged him up. 'See you in the morning,' she whispered.

Twilight rubbed his head against her.

Smiling happily, Lauren ran to the house. Her parents and Max were fast asleep. Reaching her room, Lauren changed quickly into her nightdress and looked out of her bedroom window. Twilight was standing by the fence.

''Night, Twilight,' she said softly.

Twilight glanced up at the window, almost as if he had heard her. She smiled and then, closing the curtains, got into bed.

'Isn't it cold today?' Jessica Parker, Lauren's friend, said the next day as she and Lauren and Mel Cassidy got off the school bus.

Lauren nodded and pulled her coat closer around her. The sky was grey and full of rain clouds. She thought longingly of the long hot days of summer – the picnic rides, taking the ponies to the creek in the woods – and sighed. 'I wish it could be summer all year round.'

'Do you?' Mel said in surprise. 'But if it was then we wouldn't have frosty mornings when it's cold but the sun's shining and we wouldn't have snow.'

'I guess,' Lauren said. 'And it's fun going to indoor horse shows in the winter.' She thought about her cousin, Hannah. 'It never gets really cold in Florida, where Hannah lives.'

'She's arriving tomorrow afternoon, isn't she?' Jess said.

Lauren nodded. 'She's got a four-day weekend like we have with Monday and Friday off school. You'll have to come round and meet her. I bet she'd really like to see Shadow and Sandy. She's crazy about ponies.' Shadow and Sandy were Mel and Jessica's ponies.

'Sounds like we'll get on then,' Jessica grinned.

'Hey, I've had an idea!' Mel exclaimed. 'Why don't we do a pony party to welcome her? We could get the ponies looking really great, make a banner and do food with a pony theme.'

'Yeah!' Lauren said, loving the idea. 'It

was Hannah's birthday last week so we could make a cake too. I'm going to get her a present after school today.'

'We could come over and get everything ready tomorrow morning before she arrives,' Jessica suggested.

'Cool!' Lauren grinned round at her friends. This was going to be so much fun!

★

★ ★★

CHAPTER

Two

Mrs Foster picked Lauren up after school. 'How was your day, honey?' she asked as Lauren got into the car.

'OK, thanks,' Lauren said, dumping her school bag down by her feet. 'I've got loads of homework though. I can't believe the teachers have given us so much. We've only got two extra days at the weekend.'

'You'd better get it done tonight before Hannah arrives tomorrow,' her mum said. She began to drive to the shops. 'Now, I thought we could buy her a book for her birthday. Shall we call in at Mrs Fontana's bookshop?'

'Oh yes,' Lauren said eagerly. 'I bet Mrs Fontana will suggest something good.'

Mrs Fontana was one of the few people in the world who knew about Twilight. She had once owned a secret unicorn too and when Lauren had first got Twilight, Mrs Fontana had given her an amazing old book called *The Life of a Unicorn*. It had lots of information about unicorns and the magic land they came from which was called Arcadia.

The Life of a Unicorn

As Lauren thought about Mrs Fontana,
she suddenly realized that she hadn't seen
her for a while. She began to work back
in her head. It must be about six weeks
since she'd last been into the bookshop
or had met Mrs Fontana in the woods at
night. Weird. When she had first got
Twilight, they had always been searching
Mrs Fontana out to ask her for advice
on how to use his magic to best help

people and other animals but now they seemed to be much better at working out how to use his magic themselves.

Looking out of the window, Lauren reflected on all the things she and Twilight had been up to since she had last seen Mrs Fontana. They hadn't had any really big adventures, just a few small ones. A few weeks ago, Mel's cat, Sparkle, had gone missing. Lauren and Twilight had used his seeing magic to look into a rock of rose quartz and had discovered that Sparkle was stuck in a tree in the woods. They had flown to rescue her and returned her safely. Then another night they had used Twilight's ability to untangle things with his horn and had freed a young terrier dog they had found trapped in a bramble thicket with an injured leg. Twilight had used his magic to heal the dog's leg and he had run home. Then, only the other night, they had helped Max by flying to fetch a school book that he'd left in his friend's garden. They hadn't needed to ask Mrs Fontana's advice for any of those things.

Mrs Foster turned off the road and drove into a parking space in front of a row of shops. Mrs Fontana's shop had a bow window with a brown and gold wooden sign above it that read: MRS FONTANA'S NEW AND SECOND-HAND BOOKS.

'You go on ahead of me. I need to get

some dog food and call in at the chemist,' Mrs Foster said. 'I'll come and find you at Mrs Fontana's when I'm done.'

'OK.' Lauren ran over to the bookshop.

As she pushed open the door, a bell tinkled and Mrs Fontana's black-and-white

dog scampered across the faded
rose-patterned carpet to meet her.

'Hi, Walter,' Lauren said, leaning down
to tickle him under the chin. She
straightened up and looked around. There
were the usual piles of books everywhere
and comfy chairs to sit on, but there was
no sign of Mrs Fontana. Breathing in the
familiar smell of blackcurrants that always
seemed to hang in the air of the
bookshop, Lauren made her way down to
the children and young adult section.

As she reached it, she heard the sound
of coughing. Mrs Fontana came out from
the storeroom at the back of the shop.
Not noticing Lauren, she leaned on a
bookshelf and drew in a painful breath

before coughing again. Lauren felt very worried. The old lady's face was very pale and her wrinkles looked much deeper than normal. She had lost weight and her hand, holding on to the bookshelf, trembled.

'Mrs Fontana?' Lauren said.

Mrs Fontana looked round. Seeing Lauren, she quickly straightened up and smiled. 'Lauren! I didn't realize you were here. I didn't hear the shop bell go. What a lovely surprise.'

'I came to buy a book for my cousin,' Lauren said. She frowned. 'Mum told me you haven't been well.'

'I'm fine, my dear,' Mrs Fontana replied, stifling a cough. 'Just feeling my age a bit.'

'If you're ill, why don't we get Twilight to heal you?' Lauren said. Twilight's horn had magical healing properties. 'Or we could get some water from the Waterfall of Stars?' she asked. 'Maybe if you had some of that you might feel better?' A little while ago, she and Twilight had collected some precious magical water from a waterfall just outside Arcadia. They had used it to make Shadow better when he'd been ill.

'No,' Mrs Fontana said. She looked at Lauren, her blue eyes wise but sad. 'Lauren, I cannot be helped by unicorn magic. I am ill because I'm old. That is all. There is nothing you can do to help.'

Lauren stared at her. 'We must be able to.'

Mrs Fontana came over and took her hands. 'Not this time. Time passes. People get older.' Her voice softened. 'That's just the way things are, Lauren. You must use Twilight's magic to help people and animals who really need your help, not waste it fighting a battle that can't be won.'

Lauren looked at her. She couldn't believe she and Twilight couldn't help Mrs Fontana feel better.

Mrs Fontana squeezed her hands. 'I have something for you. Wait here.'

She walked slowly into the storeroom and a few minutes later returned with a wooden box. Its edges were trimmed with faded gold and it had a lock with a small golden key in it. Lauren looked at it in surprise.

'This is for you.' Mrs Fontana placed it in Lauren's hands. As she did so, the lock seemed to click faintly. Curiously, Lauren went to turn the key. What was inside?

'No, my dear!' Mrs Fontana said quickly. 'Don't open it yet.'

'You mean to wait until I get home?' Lauren said, puzzled.

Mrs Fontana shook her head, and for a moment her blue eyes seemed to twinkle with the same sparkle they always had. 'You must open it when the time is right,' she said mysteriously.

'But when will that be?' Lauren asked.

'You will know, my dear. You'll know,' Mrs Fontana replied. She looked at the box. 'Look after it for me,' she said softly.

Lauren glanced down. The box was heavy. She was longing to know what was inside it.

'Now,' Mrs Fontana said, her voice becoming brisk. 'You said you want a book for your cousin? This is the one who likes horses, is it?'

Lauren nodded and for the next five minutes, Mrs Fontana showed her different books. Lauren had just chosen one on preparing horses for shows, when the shop door opened and Mrs Foster came in.

'Hello,' she smiled as she walked towards them. 'How are you, Mrs Fontana?'

'Not too bad, thank you,' the old lady replied.

'Have you chosen a book, Lauren?' Mrs Foster asked.

'Yes, this one.' Lauren picked up the book and the chest.

'What have you got there?' Mrs Foster asked, looking curiously at the chest.

'It's just something I've given her,' Mrs Fontana put in quickly. 'There are a few bits and pieces inside I think she might like.'

'Well, that's very kind of you, Mrs Fontana,' Mrs Foster said.

Mrs Fontana smiled at Lauren. 'My pleasure. I'm sure I'm putting them in the right hands.' She walked slowly over to the till and rang up the book.

Just then the door opened and a woman in her thirties came in. She had short brown hair and a slightly anxious expression. When she saw Mrs Fontana at the till, she frowned and hurried over.

'Aunt Margaret, I told you not to tire yourself out serving customers. What happened to the notice I put on the door saying we were closed?'

'I took it down,' Mrs Fontana said calmly. 'I'm fine, Catherine.' She turned to Lauren. 'This is my niece, Catherine Thomas. She's been helping me run the shop for the last few weeks. Catherine, this is Lauren and Alice Foster.'

'We met last time I was in,' Mrs Foster said.

Catherine smiled quickly at her. 'Yes, I remember.' She turned her attention back to Mrs Fontana. 'Please, Aunt Margaret. Sit down and rest.'

'All right, Catherine,' Mrs Fontana told

her. She turned to Lauren. 'Say hi to
Twilight for me.'

Their eyes met.

'I will,' Lauren promised. 'Bye, Mrs
Fontana.'

'Goodbye, my dear.' The old lady
turned away.

Catherine put a hand on her shoulder.

'Come and sit down, Aunt Margaret,' Lauren heard her say softly.

Lauren took one last look at Mrs Fontana and then followed her mum out of the shop.

Mrs Foster looked worried as she unlocked the car. 'Mrs Fontana didn't look well.'

'I know,' Lauren replied. 'She was coughing lots.'

'I'm glad she's got her niece to help her,' Mrs Fontana said. She glanced across as Lauren got into the car and put the box on her knee. 'What's inside the chest?' she asked curiously.

Lauren hesitated. She didn't want to tell her mum that she wasn't supposed to look yet. 'Oh, just some stuff,' she said vaguely, 'about horses.'

'Well, it was lovely of Mrs Fontana to give you it.' Her mum started the engine. 'She seems to have a real soft spot for you. First that other book and now this.'

Lauren looked at the box. What was inside? As she held it, a tingle of magic seemed to creep over her fingers. Lauren was sure that whatever was in the box was something about unicorns. If only she could open it. But she had to wait. How long for though? When *would* it be the right time?

Mrs Fontana's voice seemed to echo in her ears. '*You'll know, my dear. You'll know.*'

CHAPTER
Three

Twilight was waiting for Lauren beside the gate of his paddock. She hurried down the path towards him, the chest in her arms. 'Hi, Twilight!'

Twilight pricked up his ears and stared at the box.

'Mrs Fontana gave it to me.' Lauren climbed over the gate. 'But I'm not allowed to open it yet.'

Twilight touched the box with his nose. He breathed in deeply and looked at Lauren. She wished she could tell what he was thinking.

'I'll come out as soon as I can tonight,' she promised. 'We can talk about it properly then.' She rubbed his neck. 'I'll go and get out of my school things, then we can go for a ride in the woods. We won't be able to go out for very long though because I've got loads of homework to do.' She kissed his nose. 'I'll get changed as quickly as I can!'

It didn't take Lauren long to put her horsey jeans on. She brushed Twilight over, tacked him up and they set off into the woods. 'Let's go to the banks,' Lauren said to him.

There was an area of the woods which had lots of steep banks and little hills. Lauren loved riding Twilight up and down them. Sometimes she and Jessica and Mel put small jumps at the bottom of the less steep hills.

As she drew near, she heard the sound of familiar voices.

It was Lauren's friends, Jo-Ann and Grace, from Orchard Stables. They were a few years older than her but she got on really well with them. She clicked her tongue and let Twilight trot on.

'Hi, Lauren!' Grace called as Twilight entered the clearing. She was sitting on her grey mare, Apple. Jo-Ann, her best friend, was riding up and down the hills on Beauty, her bay pony.

'Hi!' Lauren called back. She rode over. 'How's Currant?'

Currant, Apple's foal, was also a secret unicorn. He belonged to Grace and she

was also his Unicorn Friend. She couldn't ride him yet because he was too young but she often turned him into a unicorn and played with him at night-time. 'He's fine,' Grace grinned. 'We've been having lots of fun.' She dropped her voice. 'He's getting loads better at flying now, Lauren . . .' She broke off as Jo-Ann and Beauty cantered over.

'Do you want to join in with us, Lauren?' Jo-Ann asked, reining Beauty in beside Twilight. 'We were going to time ourselves to see how fast we could get round four of the hills.'

'Cool,' Lauren said. She'd have loved to have carried on talking to Grace about unicorn stuff but they would have to wait. 'Of course Twilight and I will join in. Which hills are they?'

Jo-Ann pointed out a short course. The three girls took it in turns to canter round the course and time each other. Jo-Ann always won, but that was no surprise. She was a very daring rider and Beauty was very fast. Lauren didn't mind. It was just fun joining in.

After going round three times each they gave the ponies a break. 'Your cousin, Hannah, is coming tomorrow, isn't she?' Grace said.

'That's right,' Lauren replied.

'Mum told me she's going to borrow Magpie,' Grace went on. Her mum owned Orchard Stables. 'Do you want me to bring him over tomorrow, late afternoon? I can ride Apple and lead him.'

'Yes please!' Lauren said. 'I bet Hannah's going to love having him to look after and ride. We haven't told her about it yet. It's going to be a surprise.'

'Magpie'll enjoy it too,' Grace said. 'He's a bit lively for the riding school so he doesn't get used much but your mum said that Hannah's a really good rider so I'm sure she'll be able to handle him.'

'She's brilliant,' Lauren nodded. 'She's been riding since she was three and she does lots of showjumping.'

Jo-Ann shortened her reins. 'Come on! Let's have another go at the course!

Why don't we all go round together this time?'

'OK,' Lauren grinned. She clicked her tongue and Twilight leapt forward eagerly with the others.

After supper that night, Lauren helped her mum get the spare room ready for Hannah. They made up the bed and then Lauren put some of her favourite pony books on to the bedside table together with a china ornament of a rearing stallion. She placed the book for Hannah's birthday, all wrapped up, on the bed. 'I can't wait till Hannah gets here,' she told her mum.

'It'll be so good to see her again,' Mrs

Foster said. 'I can't believe it's been a whole year since we saw her last.'

'We're going to have so much fun,' Lauren said happily.

'In which case you'd better get your homework done tonight!' Mrs Foster reminded her.

Lauren sighed. 'OK, I'll go and do it now.'

She went into her room and got out her books. They were doing all about different types of rock in Geography and she had to answer a page of questions on rock formations. Lauren groaned as she picked up her pen. Rocks were so dull. Thinking about ponies was much more fun!

★

Twilight was waiting for Lauren
when she crept out of the house that
evening. He whinnied softly when he
saw her.

Lauren quickly said the words of the
Turning Spell:

> '*Twilight Star, Twilight Star,*
> *Twinkling high above so far.*
> *Shining light, shining bright,*
> *Will you grant my wish tonight?*
> *Let my little horse forlorn*
> *Be at last a unicorn!*'

There was a bright purple flash and
Twilight transformed into a unicorn.
'Hi,' he said, stepping forward.

Lauren hugged him. It always felt so good to hear him speak.

'I wonder what's in that chest Mrs Fontana gave you?' Twilight said, nuzzling her. 'It smelled of magic when you showed it to me before.'

'I bet it's something to do with unicorns,' Lauren replied. 'But what?'

'When can you open it?' Twilight asked.

'That's the thing. I don't know. Mrs
Fontana just said I wasn't to open it until
the time was right.' Lauren frowned in
frustration. 'You know, sometimes I wish
Mrs Fontana wouldn't talk in riddles so
much! She always does that if we ask her
advice about magic too!'

Twilight nuzzled her shoulder. 'That's
just her way. I think she likes making us
figure stuff out for ourselves. Come on,
let's go flying,' he said. 'I want to jump
over the treetops again!'

'Me too!' Lauren grinned. She got on
to his back and they cantered upward
into the starry sky.

CHAPTER

Four

'Can I have the shampoo please, Lauren?' Mel called the following morning. Mel, Lauren and Jessica were all washing their ponies' tails to make them look as beautiful as possible.

Lauren chucked her the bottle of shampoo. As she let go of Twilight's tail, he flicked it from side to side. Water droplets sprayed everywhere.

Lauren, Jessica and Mel squealed as the droplets covered their jeans.

Lauren put her hands on her hips. 'Thanks, Twilight!'

Twilight looked round cheekily and snorted.

Picking up a towel, she dried his tail and then wiped off the water droplets from his back. She'd groomed him really well and his grey coat was soft and smooth and his mane was lying neatly on one side of his neck.

'I guess we'd better clean up,' Lauren said as Mel washed the shampoo off Shadow's tail.

'And then we can put the banner up,' Jessica said.

'And get the food out,' Mel put in.

The three of them bustled about. They'd made a banner first thing that morning and had written *Happy Birthday, Hannah!* on it. They had also made pony-shaped biscuits and Mrs Foster had made a cake. Soon everything was set out, the ponies were looking beautiful and the biscuits and cakes and bowls of cut-up carrot and apple pieces were all laid out on a table by Twilight's stable.

'Now all we need is Hannah,' Mel said, looking round happily.

There was the sound of a car turning into the drive. 'I bet that's her!' Lauren exclaimed. Lauren's dad had left earlier to fetch Hannah from the airport. 'Come on!'

They hurried up the path that led back to the house. 'Hannah!' Lauren yelled as a tall girl with brown hair got out of the car.

She raced over to give her cousin a hug but as she got near she slowed down. Hannah looked really different. Her wild, curly hair had been cut and straightened and instead of being in a messy ponytail, it now fell sleekly to her shoulders. She was also wearing make-up and her nails were painted silver. In the past, she had always worn jeans and trainers but now she had a skirt and ankle boots on. Her warm, friendly smile was the same though.

'Hi, Lauren,' she said.

Lauren didn't know whether to hug her or not. Hannah looked so grown-up. Luckily Hannah made the decision for her. She stepped forward and embraced Lauren. 'It's great to see you again.'

'You too,' Lauren said, hugging her back.

Mrs Foster came over. 'You look great,

Hannah,' she said. 'I like your hair like that.'

'Thanks, Auntie Alice,' Hannah said, kissing her.

Lauren suddenly remembered she had introductions to make. She swung round. 'Hannah, these are my friends, Mel Cassidy and Jessica Parker.'

'Hi,' Jessica and Mel said together.

Hannah smiled at them. 'Nice to meet you both.'

'We've got something to show you!' Lauren told her. 'It's by the stables!'

She led the way down the path with Hannah following.

The ponies looked round as they heard the footsteps on the gravel.

Twilight pricked up his ears and whinnied. The banner fluttered in the breeze.

'Oh wow!' Hannah said, glancing quickly at the ponies and then looking at the banner. 'It's a birthday banner.' She smiled round at them. 'Thanks, guys!'

'Lauren, Jessica and Mel have been

working on getting a welcome party
ready for you all morning,' Mrs Foster
said. 'Come and have a drink and a
biscuit or a slice of cake, Hannah. I bet
you're ready for something after your
journey.'

'I sure am,' Hannah agreed. She went
over to the table. 'It all looks delicious.'

'Help yourself,' Mrs Foster said.

Hannah poured a drink and took a
biscuit. Twilight whinnied again but
she didn't look round. Lauren felt
slightly put out. Hannah hadn't said
anything about him and Shadow and
Sandy – and they were all looking
gorgeous.

'Twilight's the pony that's whinnying,'

she said, trying to draw Hannah's attention to the ponies. 'He's mine.'

Hannah glanced round briefly. 'He's lovely, Lauren.' She turned back to the table. 'Can I have a slice of cake as well please, Auntie Alice?'

Lauren stared at her. Hannah had barely even looked at Twilight!

'Mel's pony is the darker dapple grey. He's called Shadow,' she persevered as Mel and Jessica took some carrots over for the eager ponies. 'And the palomino is Sandy. He's Jessica's pony. Well, Jess officially shares him with Samantha, her stepsister, but Samantha doesn't ride much now. She's not so interested in ponies any more.'

'No, me neither,' Hannah said casually. 'I haven't been to the stables near me for ages.'

If she'd said she'd been walking on the moon, Lauren couldn't have been more surprised. She stared at her cousin. 'What?'

Hannah shrugged. 'I've just got really busy with other stuff, I guess.' She looked towards the three ponies. 'I don't really have time for all that pony stuff now. I like going round to my friends' houses and listening to music, or we go to the mall. And . . .' She blushed slightly. 'I've got a boyfriend, so I see him quite a bit.'

Lauren couldn't believe it. Hannah wasn't into ponies! But it had been all she'd ever been interested in. However, before she could say anything, Hannah had turned to Mrs Foster. 'So where's Max?' she asked, looking round.

'Playing. He's really into skateboarding at the moment and spends all his time with his friends, Leo and Stephen,' Mrs Foster said. 'He'll be back for lunch. And then you'll get to meet Buddy too.'

'I bet Max has really grown,' Hannah said. 'I can't believe he's eight now!'

Lauren walked slowly over to Mel and Jessica who were standing by the ponies.

'Did Hannah just say she isn't into ponies?' Jess hissed.

Lauren nodded. Her brain couldn't seem to take it in. How *could* Hannah not like ponies any more? 'I just don't get it,' she said, feeling bewildered. 'Hannah's always been so pony-crazy.'

'I guess people change,' Mel said.

'Sam's the same,' Jess said. 'She never wants to do stuff with Sandy any more.'

Lauren thought about the pony books in Hannah's room and the book she'd

bought her as a birthday present and groaned inwardly. Twilight seemed to sense her dismay and stepped forward to nuzzle her.

'I'm going to take Hannah inside and show her where her room is,' Mrs Foster called.

'Maybe Jess and I should go back to my house for a while,' Mel said to Lauren.

'Yeah, that's a good idea,' said Jess. 'You and Hannah must have loads of catching up to do. We'll come back tomorrow.'

'OK,' said Lauren. She had a feeling her friends were a bit disappointed at Hannah's lack of excitement over the pony welcome party. She was too. She'd imagined them all spending the rest of the morning together, riding Twilight and Shadow and Sandy in the field. 'See you.'

Leaving Mel and Jessica to tack up Shadow and Sandy, she went after her mum and Hannah. What was Hannah going to say when she saw all the pony things in the bedroom she was staying in?

Hannah was looking round the room with Mrs Foster when Lauren joined them. She didn't even mention the pony books and ornament but she did open the present.

'Hey, a book on showing!' Hannah said as she pulled it out of the paper. She tried to sound pleased. 'Thanks, Auntie Alice. Thanks, Lauren.'

Lauren felt a blush warm her cheeks. 'I didn't realize you'd gone off ponies,' she said awkwardly.

'We can always change it,' Mrs Foster said.

'No, it's fine,' Hannah said politely.

Mrs Foster headed to the door. 'I'll go and put lunch on. You two stay and chat. I'll call you when it's ready.'

Hannah began to unpack her case. There were some magazines at the top of it.

'Do you like Leeza Lemarq?' Hannah said to Lauren, pointing to a singer on the front of one of the magazines. 'She's got such a cool voice. I love her stuff. I'm into loads of different music at the moment – Catz 'n' Dogz, Gina Natina, The Basement Belles. They're all great.' She smiled enthusiastically. 'I've got loads of CDs with me. We can listen to them.'

Lauren nodded but she wasn't really into sitting round and listening to music. She liked having it on as she did other stuff but she didn't know much about different bands or singers.

'I've brought my make-up and hair straighteners with me,' Hannah went on. 'And my set of nail varnishes.' She smiled. 'I'll do a make-over on you if you like.'

'Thanks,' Lauren said slowly. She could hardly believe this was Hannah. The Hannah she remembered always had messy hair and dirt under her bitten nails.

'And maybe we could go shopping together and see a movie,' Hannah went on.

'Yeah, maybe.' Lauren's heart sank. So much for them doing loads of pony things together. Suddenly she remembered about Grace bringing Magpie round that afternoon. 'Um, I've just got to go and speak to Mum,' she said quickly. 'I'll be back in a few minutes.'

'OK,' Hannah said easily. 'I'll get on with unpacking.'

Lauren hurried downstairs. She'd better ask her mum to ring up Grace and say they didn't need Magpie.

But to her surprise her mum said no. 'Hannah's only just arrived. Maybe when she's settled in she'll decide she wants to ride after all. We've arranged to borrow Magpie now so we might as well have him here.'

'But she said she doesn't like ponies any more,' Lauren said.

Mrs Foster looked thoughtful. 'I can't imagine Hannah has really changed that much. She might seem to have changed but I'll be very surprised if the old pony-loving Hannah isn't somewhere underneath there still.'

Lauren hesitated. Was the old pony-mad Hannah really still there? Thinking of the grown-up fourteen-year-old upstairs it

was hard to imagine it, but maybe her mum was right and Hannah just needed to be reminded of how much she liked ponies.

Perhaps if I can get her riding Twilight then she'll start to remember. We can groom him together afterwards and clean his tack. That'll be fun, Lauren thought. *And then*

Grace will arrive with Magpie and we can settle him into his stable together.

Determination filled her. *I bet I can do this*, she decided. *By the end of today I'm going to have reminded Hannah of just how much fun ponies can be!*

CHAPTER

Five

Mrs Foster had cooked jacket
potatoes for lunch and there
were also big bowls of baked beans,
cheese, ham and salad.

'This is delicious,' Hannah said.

'I love jacket potatoes,' Max said,
helping himself to a big spoonful of
cheese.

'Woof!' said Buddy as a few pieces of

grated cheese escaped from Max's spoon and fell on to the floor. He gobbled them up.

Lauren grinned. 'I think Buddy likes this lunch too!'

'He's gorgeous,' Hannah said, patting him.

'So what are your plans this afternoon?' Mrs Foster asked Lauren and Hannah.

'I thought we could ride Twilight in the field,' Lauren suggested. 'He's really brilliant to ride. We could put up some jumps.' She looked hopefully at her cousin. Hannah had always loved jumping.

Hannah didn't look too keen. 'Well,

I don't mind watching you, Lauren.' She smoothed her dark hair. 'But I don't really want to ride myself. If I put a riding hat on it'll make my hair go frizzy and it takes forever to get it straight.'

Lauren stared. Hannah was turning down a chance to ride just because it would mess up her hair! For a moment she felt a flicker of doubt about her plan. Maybe Hannah really *had* changed completely.

'Well, why don't you watch and see how you feel?' Mrs Foster said.

Lauren nodded. She wasn't going to give up on her plan. Not yet, anyway. 'I bet you'll want to ride when you see him jumping,' she told Hannah.

Hannah looked awkward. 'Lauren, I . . .'

But Lauren wouldn't let her finish. 'We're going to have so much fun!' she interrupted.

I hope, she added silently to herself.

After clearing away the lunch dishes, Lauren and Hannah went outside. 'I love this place,' Hannah said, looking round at the farm surrounded by the wooded mountains. Mr Foster was working on a tractor in a nearby field. He waved at them and they waved back.

'I love living here too,' Lauren said. 'It's great.' She seized the chance to turn the conversation towards ponies. 'All my

friends here ride. There's a creek in the
woods – we take the ponies to paddle in
it in the summer – and there's lots of
hills to ride up and down and ditches to
jump and some great tracks for cantering
on. It's so much fun!'

Hannah nodded. 'Yeah, I used to like
doing pony stuff too.'

She didn't sound very interested but

Lauren soldiered on. 'You'll have to meet my friends, Grace and Jo-Ann. They're fourteen and they still love horses. We often get together and go out for rides.'

'Oh, right,' Hannah said, not sounding too interested.

Lauren felt a wave of frustration but she pushed it down. 'Come on, let's go and tack Twilight up,' she said. She fetched Twilight's tack, hoping Hannah would offer to help her saddle up but Hannah just stood back. Lauren decided to tell her about Magpie. Maybe the thought of having a pony of her own for a few days would make her change. 'Grace, one of the friends I was just telling you about, is bringing a pony over later,' she said. 'He's called Magpie. Mum arranged to borrow him for the next few days so you can ride him.'

Hannah looked uncomfortable. 'Oh.'

'He's lovely to ride,' Lauren went on eagerly. 'Quite lively but you'll have a great time on him. We'll be able to go into the woods and . . .'

'Sorry, Lauren,' Hannah interrupted. 'I don't mean to be horrid but I don't want to ride.'

'But . . .' Lauren began.

'No, Lauren!' Hannah said, beginning to sound cross. 'I know you're still into ponies but I'm not. I've grown out of them, so stop trying to pressurize me and make me do stuff I don't want to!'

There was a silence.

Hannah drew in a deep breath. 'I'm going to go and read in my room,' she said. 'I'll see you when you've finished riding.'

She hurried away.

Lauren and Twilight stared after her. Lauren felt awful. She hadn't meant to make Hannah cross and unhappy. She'd only been trying to get her interested in ponies again.

Twilight whickered uncertainly. Lauren desperately wanted to talk to him. 'Oh, Twilight,' she said. 'Let's go to the secret glade so I can turn you into a unicorn and we can talk.'

Twilight nodded.

Lauren quickly finished saddling him up and they headed off.

The secret glade was a small clearing deep in the woods. It was hidden at the end of an overgrown path and was one of Lauren's favourite places in the world. It always felt very magical. Purple flowers dotted the short grass. In summer, butterflies flew through the air and at night-time fireflies lit up the darkness like tiny flashing lights. It was the one place where it felt safe to turn Twilight into a unicorn in the daytime. No one else ever seemed to go there.

As soon as they reached it, Lauren said the Turning Spell.

'What's happened?' Twilight asked as

soon as he could talk. 'I thought you said
Hannah loved ponies, Lauren.'

'She used to,' Lauren said, rubbing her
hand across her forehead. 'But now she
says she's outgrown them.'

Twilight looked at Lauren with
alarmed eyes. 'You won't ever outgrow
me, will you?'

'No!' Lauren hugged him fiercely.
'Never! I promise!'

Twilight snorted in relief.

'Oh, Twilight!' Lauren said, thinking of
Hannah with her sleek hair, carefully
painted nails, music magazines and
boyfriend. 'Hannah used to be so nice.'
She caught herself. 'Well, I suppose she
still is nice, but I wish she still liked

ponies. I thought she might do deep down, so that's why I was trying to get her to ride and do stuff.'

Twilight looked at her. 'It didn't seem to work.'

'No,' Lauren sighed. 'It didn't. I feel bad for upsetting her, particularly when she's only just arrived.'

Twilight pushed her gently with his nose. 'You were only trying to help, Lauren.'

Lauren stroked him. Twilight always knew the right thing to say to make her feel better. 'I'm so glad I've got you,' she whispered.

'And I'm glad I've got you,' he snorted.

Lauren rested her head against his neck. They stood there for a long moment.

At last Lauren sighed. 'I guess we'd better go home. I should find Hannah and go and listen to some music or something with her.'

'Will you turn me into a unicorn later?' Twilight said eagerly.

'Of course!' Lauren smiled.

She said the Undoing Spell and Twilight turned back into a pony. Lauren mounted and they headed back to Granger's Farm.

When Lauren got back, she went into the house. Hannah was in the lounge. She'd changed out of her skirt into a pair of trousers and was watching a music programme on TV. 'Hi,' she said quietly.

'Hi,' Lauren replied, feeling awkward.

'Look, I'm sorry about snapping earlier,' Hannah said. 'I just felt you weren't listening to me. You were trying to make me do stuff I didn't want to do.'

'I'm sorry too,' Lauren said. 'I just thought it might be fun to do some pony stuff. I didn't mean to upset you.'

'That's OK. I'm just not into ponies any more.' Hannah looked at the telly. 'Shall I turn this off?'

'No, it's fine. I don't mind watching it with you,' Lauren replied.

Hannah smiled. 'Cool.'

Lauren sat and watched the programme. It was OK, she supposed, but she would far rather have been outside with Twilight. She didn't know any of the bands playing, although Hannah seemed to know lots about them. As it finished, she glanced at her watch. Grace would be arriving any moment.

'I should go back out,' she said, standing up. 'My friend's coming round with that pony I told you about.' She looked hopefully at Hannah. Surely she couldn't resist coming out to see Magpie?

But it seemed as if Hannah could. She picked up one of the magazines that was lying beside her. 'OK. See you later.'

Lauren sighed. If only Hannah would come with her. She left the house and

reached Twilight's field just as Grace
came riding through the wood on Apple.
Magpie, a glossy young piebald pony, was
jogging beside Apple, his ears pricked up,
his dark eyes curious.

'Hi!' Grace waved.

Lauren waved back and went over to
take Magpie's reins. He pulled forward
excitedly, almost knocking Lauren over.

'Sorry, he's only young and he's not
used to strange places,' Grace said as
Lauren steadied him. 'It'll do him good
to be here for a few nights.' She looked
round. 'Where's your cousin then?'

Lauren felt embarrassed. She didn't
want Grace to feel put out about having
brought Magpie over for nothing. 'Oh,

she's just inside at the moment,' she said. 'She'll be out soon.'

Grace smiled. 'I bet she'll love Magpie. Oh well, I'd better be getting back. Mum's been out at a show all day with some of the ponies and I said I'd be there to help her unload and feed them. Maybe we can all go for a ride some time? You, me, Jo-Ann and your cousin. Mel and Jess too, if they want to come?'

'Yeah, sounds great,' Lauren said vaguely. 'Thank you so much for bringing Magpie round. I'll give you a ring.'

'Cool!' Grace said. 'See you!' She rode off on Apple.

Lauren led Magpie over to the fence.

Twilight whickered and came over and the two ponies touched noses. Magpie seemed to relax slightly as Twilight breathed softly at him.

'Guess I'll be riding you as well as Twilight for the next few days if Hannah doesn't want to ride you,' Lauren said to Magpie. A picture of Hannah sitting in the lounge reading her magazines came into her mind. Fun as it would be to have two ponies to ride, it would have been even better if she and Hannah could have gone riding together.

I wish Hannah hadn't changed so much, she thought wistfully.

CHAPTER
Six

L auren laughed in delight as she and Twilight swooped over the treetops later that night.

'This is fun!' Twilight said.

Lauren wrapped her hands in his mane. With the stars whizzing by, she could almost forget all about Hannah not liking ponies any more.

Suddenly her eyes caught a flash of

yellow in the trees beneath and she heard the faint yap of a dog.

'Twilight! It's Mrs Fontana and Walter! Mrs Fontana must be feeling better if she's out walking in the woods. Let's go and see them.'

Twilight swooped down.

Mrs Fontana was walking slowly along the path. She was looking through the trees, almost as if she was searching for something. Walter was not bounding on ahead as he usually did, but was staying close to her side.

Twilight whinnied and Mrs Fontana glanced up. For a moment a look of delight crossed her face but then her shoulders seemed to sag and the delight instantly faded. Lauren stared at the old lady in surprise. It was almost as if Mrs Fontana had been expecting to see someone else instead of them.

'Hi, Mrs Fontana,' she called.

Mrs Fontana smiled with her usual warm smile. 'Hello, my dears,' she said as Twilight flew down and landed.

'How are you?' Lauren asked.

'Oh, I'm as well as can be expected.' Mrs Fontana coughed and pulled her mustard-yellow shawl around her. Lauren looked at her in concern. Mrs Fontana didn't seem any better. So what was she doing out in the cold November night?

'You look so lovely flying together,' Mrs Fontana said with a strange, sad smile. 'Sometimes you really remind me of my old unicorn, Twilight. He was called Midnight Star and had a silver horn like yours. His mane reached to the floor and he had the deepest, darkest eyes I've ever seen.'

Lauren looked at her. There was something she'd wanted to know ever since she'd first found out Mrs Fontana had once had a unicorn but she'd never found the right moment to ask. 'Mrs Fontana, why did you let your unicorn go back to Arcadia? Why did you say goodbye to him?'

Mrs Fontana paused before answering. 'Things change,' she said at last. 'The time came for me to let him go.'

Twilight whickered anxiously.

'You'll understand one day,' Mrs
Fontana said.

But Lauren knew she never would.
'I couldn't do it,' she breathed. 'I couldn't
say goodbye to Twilight. Not ever.'

'It was hard,' Mrs Fontana said, her
eyes clouding with memories. 'The
hardest thing I've ever done but it had to

happen. Still, I know that one day we will meet again and then we will never be parted.'

'You'll meet again?' Lauren said, confused. 'But how? And when?'

'How and when are not questions I can answer, my dear,' Mrs Fontana replied softly. 'But enough about me. Are you having a good time now your cousin is here?'

Lauren sighed. 'Not really.'

'Hannah doesn't like riding any more,' Twilight said.

'Oh dear,' Mrs Fontana sighed. 'And you were so looking forward to doing pony stuff with her.'

'I wish people didn't have to change,

Mrs Fontana,' Lauren said wistfully.

Mrs Fontana looked at her. 'Oh, usually you find that people haven't really changed deep down, however old and grown-up they get. I don't think Hannah will really have changed. I think she probably just needs reminding of how much she loves ponies.'

'My mum said the same thing,' Lauren said. 'But it's not true. I've been trying to get Hannah to do pony stuff but all she wants is to sit inside. Can you think of anything, Mrs Fontana?'

'Lauren's been trying really hard,' Twilight added.

'Hmm.' Mrs Fontana frowned thoughtfully. 'Perhaps you've been trying *too* hard, Lauren. Most people don't like feeling they're being forced into things. Is there any way you could get Hannah to do stuff without it seeming like you were trying to *make* her like ponies again? Then she might remember how much she really loves them.'

Lauren thought hard. 'Hannah's very kind,' she replied slowly. 'I guess if I couldn't look after Twilight and Magpie for some reason, she might offer to look after them for me.'

'I know!' Twilight snorted. 'Why don't you pretend you're sick, Lauren?'

'Yeah!' Lauren looked at him in excitement. 'Perhaps I could pretend to be ill tomorrow morning. I know it would be a lie – but it would only be a little white lie and it might help.'

'I could wake her up by whinnying from my field and you could say that you don't feel well enough to get up and feed and groom me and Magpie,' Twilight put in. 'Then she might offer.'

'And if she does all that stuff, she might just realize how much she likes being round ponies!' Lauren exclaimed.

Mrs Fontana laughed. 'Sounds like you two have a new plan. You don't need me to think of anything after all.'

Lauren smiled in delight. 'Oh, Mrs Fontana, this might just work!'

Mrs Fontana coughed and her face creased with pain. 'Are you all right?' Lauren asked anxiously.

'Here, can I help?' Twilight said, reaching out with his horn.

'No, Twilight.' Mrs Fontana stepped back. 'I am old. That is all.' She coughed again. 'Go on. You two go now,' she said, her hand on her chest as if it was hurting her. 'I'm sure you want to be having fun, flying.'

'But . . .' Lauren began.

'Go,' Mrs Fontana insisted.

Lauren could tell there was no point arguing. She took hold of Twilight's mane.

'Good luck helping Hannah,' Mrs Fontana said. 'I hope you can remind her of how much she loves ponies.'

Twilight tossed his head, his silver horn glinting in the starlight.

'We'll do our best,' Lauren promised.

'I know you will. You always do. That's what makes you both so special.' Mrs Fontana smiled, but her eyes seemed sad and clouded. She put a hand lightly on

Twilight's mane and nodded gently at Lauren. 'Goodbye, my dears.'

Lauren looked at her in surprise but Twilight was already plunging into the sky. Lauren suddenly had a strange urge to stay with the old lady and not leave her. 'Goodbye, Mrs Fontana!' she called uneasily.

Mrs Fontana lifted one hand and then turned away and stepped into the trees with Walter at her side.

As Lauren looked at the suddenly empty path, her heart clenched and a hard lump of tears formed in her throat. Unhappiness swept over her in a wave.

Don't be silly, she told herself quickly, *Mrs Fontana's only stepped off the path and gone to walk among the trees like she always does.*

But something seemed different.

'Are you OK?' Twilight asked as her fingers tightened in his mane.

'Yeah,' Lauren said slowly. 'I . . . I just feel a bit strange.' She glanced down at the empty path again. 'I don't really know why.'

'I feel odd too,' Twilight admitted. 'Do you think our plan for Hannah will work?'

'I hope so,' Lauren replied. 'I bet she'll offer to help if she thinks I'm ill.'

'I'd better be careful I don't step on her toes with my hooves then, or fidget too much when she's grooming me,' Twilight said.

Lauren looked towards the farmhouse in the distance and thought of Hannah asleep in bed. Would their plan work?

CHAPTER

Seven

In the morning, Lauren was woken up
by the sound of Twilight whinnying
loudly outside. She lay in bed for a
moment, still half-asleep and trying to
get her thoughts together. She was sure
there was something she had to
remember . . .

Her eyes blinked open. Of course! She
sat up. They were putting their plan into

action. Jumping out of bed, she went to her window. Twilight was standing by the fence, neighing.

Lauren heard the sound of Hannah's door opening just along the corridor. She raced back to bed and jumped under the cover just in time.

There was a tap at the door.

'Yes,' Lauren said.

'Lauren, it's me, Hannah.' The door opened and Hannah looked round it. 'Twilight's whinnying like mad outside.'

'He must want his breakfast,' Lauren said, making her voice sound weak. 'I should get up but I don't feel well at all.'

'What's the matter? Do you want me

to get your mum?' Hannah asked, looking worried.

'No,' Lauren said quickly. 'I feel sick. If I could just lie here for a bit I might start to feel better.'

Outside Twilight whinnied again, even more loudly.

'Oh dear, I suppose I'd better get up and feed him and Magpie,' Lauren sighed. 'I guess I can always come back to bed afterwards.' She began to sit up.

'No, wait, Lauren. I can feed them for you,' Hannah offered. 'Don't get up.'

'Are you sure?' Lauren said.

'I'll be fine,' Hannah said briskly. 'You mustn't get up if you feel ill. Look, just tell me what to feed them.'

'A scoop of bran and one of pony nuts and some soaked sugar beet,' Lauren replied. 'When Magpie's eaten he can go out in the field. Oh, and,' she added as Hannah nodded and began to turn away, 'I usually groom Twilight after his breakfast, but of course you don't have to do that . . .'

'It's fine, Lauren,' Hannah interrupted. 'I can easily groom him. You just rest and get better. Don't worry about a thing. I'll go and get dressed.'

She left the room. Lauren went to the window and gave a thumbs-up sign to Twilight. He whinnied and headed for the gate.

Lauren put her dressing gown on and

then sat on the window seat and watched what was happening. She saw Hannah get to the field and start bustling about, feeding Twilight and changing his water.

As Twilight drank from the clean water bucket, he snorted and sprayed her with water droplets. Hannah smiled and pretended to scold him. Lauren felt a buzz of hope. Hannah looked like she was enjoying herself.

Hannah turned Magpie out and then she fetched the grooming kit and tied Twilight up to the fence.

As she crouched down to brush the mud off his legs with the bristly dandy brush, Twilight nudged her in the small

of her back with his nose. She almost
overbalanced. She grinned and said
something to him. He looked at her
cheekily.

Hannah straightened up and rubbed
his face. He pushed his nose against her
chest. For a moment, Hannah looked
uncertain what to do, then she smiled
and gave him a quick hug.

'Well done, Twilight!' Lauren whispered under her breath.

Hannah removed Twilight's waterproof rug and took the soft body brush out of the grooming box. As she settled down into a regular rhythm of sweeping the brush over his coat and then cleaning the bristles on a metal curry-comb, a look of happiness gradually settled on her face.

Twilight sighed happily and as she brushed his neck, he turned his head to rest his muzzle on her shoulder. Hannah paused and gently tickled his nose. He blinked up at her and she kissed him.

Lauren felt like shouting in delight. Twilight was doing a brilliant job at showing Hannah how great ponies were.

She jumped to her feet. She couldn't stay in her bedroom any longer. She had to go downstairs!

Pulling on her jeans and sweatshirt, she hurried outside.

Hannah was grooming Twilight. She looked round when she heard Lauren's footsteps on the path.

'How are you feeling?' she asked in concern.

'Much better,' Lauren said. She decided to take a risk. 'Thanks for helping, Hannah. You can leave me to finish stuff off here if you want.'

She held her breath as Hannah hesitated. *Please don't say yes; please don't say yes*, she thought.

Twilight snorted and nuzzled the older girl's arm.

'Well, I don't mind helping you,' Hannah said slowly. 'It's been fun doing stuff this morning.'

'Well, I'd love a hand if you don't mind,' Lauren said.

'No problem,' Hannah replied.

Lauren got another body brush and they finished grooming Twilight together and then they started on Magpie.

'Are you planning on riding this morning?' Hannah asked.

Lauren nodded. 'I'll ride Twilight first and then I guess I'll have to ride Magpie.'

'Or I suppose I could come for a ride with you,' Hannah suggested. 'Then you wouldn't have to ride both of them. I'd need to borrow a hat though.'

'I've got two,' Lauren said quickly.

Hannah patted Magpie. 'Well, why don't we do that?'

'Cool!' Lauren agreed casually but inside she was jumping up and down in delight. Twilight snorted and she knew he was really pleased too.

The two girls went inside and had a quick breakfast of toast and apple juice and then they hurried back outside. As they tacked the ponies up, Magpie fidgeted in excitement.

'He seems quite lively,' Hannah said as the piebald pony swung his head up and down. She looked slightly nervous.

'You can always ride Twilight if you want,' Lauren offered.

'No, no, I'll be fine,' she said determinedly.

As they mounted, Magpie leapt forward. Hannah tightened her reins and he shook his head.

'He'll settle down as soon as we get going,' Lauren said, hoping she was right.

But as they rode up the path to the woods, Magpie jogged and sidled sideways. Hannah tensed in the saddle and tightened her hold on his mouth. He tossed his head, trying to loosen the reins. 'Steady,' Hannah muttered, digging her knees into his sides. She looked embarrassed to be having problems.

'Maybe if you give him more rein he'll settle,' Lauren said helpfully.

'I know how to ride, Lauren,' Hannah said.

They reached the sandy track and Magpie jumped forward excitedly. Hannah pulled at his mouth. He chucked his head in the air and she lost a stirrup.

'Easy, boy!' she exclaimed as she tried to get it back.

Lauren rode Twilight up alongside the young pony, hoping to calm him, but as she did so, a rabbit shot out from the undergrowth and raced across the path.

Magpie shied violently.

'Hannah!' Lauren cried in alarm as Hannah lost her balance, the reins slipping through her fingers.

'Whoa!' Hannah gasped.

She grabbed at the reins. But she wasn't fast enough. Snatching the bit between his teeth, Magpie plunged forward and began to gallop down the track.

CHAPTER

Eight

'Hannah!' Lauren yelled as Magpie galloped around the bend in the path with Hannah struggling to stay on.

'Come on, Twilight! Quick!' Lauren exclaimed, leaning forward and urging Twilight on. He broke into a canter but Magpie was bigger and faster than Twilight and as they rounded the bend,

all they saw was the empty track ahead
of them.

Lauren's heart pounded. Hannah
obviously couldn't stop Magpie. What if
she fell off and was hurt? What if Magpie
injured himself? Oh, this was all her fault.
She should never have tried so hard to
get Hannah riding again.

'Faster!' she urged Twilight. She ducked
under some overhanging branches,
expecting at any moment to come across
Hannah lying injured on the path.

Twilight raced around the next corner
and snorted in surprise. Magpie was
standing at the side of the track with
Hannah safely on his back. She was
patting his neck and talking soothingly to

him. She had regained her stirrups and looked completely in control.

Magpie shied in surprise when he saw Twilight galloping round the corner but Hannah immediately calmed him.

'Are you OK?' Lauren demanded as Twilight slowed down.

'Fine,' Hannah called. 'Sorry for letting Magpie bolt off like that. I should have

stopped him earlier but I lost my stirrups.' She stroked Magpie's neck, her eyes glowing. 'He's a fantastic pony. So fast! And as soon as I got my reins and stirrups back, I managed to stop him. He's really responsive. I should never have tried to keep him on such a tight rein. I guess I was just feeling nervous. It was really dumb of me.'

Lauren looked at her cousin's happy face and felt a wave of relief. Hannah didn't look upset at all!

'Should we carry on?' Hannah said. 'I'd love to find somewhere to have a proper canter – with my stirrups this time!'

Lauren grinned at her. 'Sounds great to me! Come on, the track widens out just round the next bend and there're some logs to jump.'

They had a great time cantering through the woods and jumping over fallen logs. By the time they got back to the farm, Hannah's face was flushed and she was looking very happy.

'Oh, Lauren! That was the best ride!' she said as they rode back down the track to the field, the ponies now walking calmly on loose reins. 'I had so much fun! I'd forgotten how great riding could be. Can we go out again tomorrow?' She glanced at Lauren. 'Maybe we could see if your friends want to come with us?'

Twilight snorted happily and Lauren

patted him. Their plan had worked! 'Of course we can,' she told Hannah.

Hannah smiled happily and they rode back to the farm.

They spent the rest of the morning doing pony things – cleaning tack and sweeping out the tack room – before going inside for lunch.

'My nail varnish is really chipped,' Hannah said, looking ruefully at her hands as they washed up the dishes after lunch. She grinned. 'Oh well, never mind. I guess I can do it again.' She glanced at Lauren. 'I could do yours too, if you like.'

Lauren smiled back. 'OK.'

'Cool!' Hannah said. 'Let's go upstairs.'

They took it in turns to paint each
other's nails while they listened to
Hannah's music. To her surprise,
Lauren found it fun. She grinned to
herself. Looking down at the magazines
on the bed, she wondered if one day
she'd be just like Hannah and be into
bands and music and stuff. Perhaps
things always did change, just like Mrs
Fontana said. Waving her fingers in the
air to dry them, she went to the
window and looked out at the field
where Twilight and Magpie were
grazing side by side. One thing she
knew wouldn't ever change was how
much she loved ponies. She was *never*

going to need to be reminded of that!

When everyone had gone to bed that night, Lauren and Twilight went flying. 'Didn't our plan work well!' Twilight said as they soared into the sky.

'It was brilliant,' Lauren said happily. 'Hannah's been talking about going back to the riding school again when she gets home. She's not going to go quite as much as she did before but she wants to keep riding as well as hanging out at her friends' houses. I'm so glad!' She hugged him. 'You were great when she came down to the field in the morning.'

Twilight gave a pleased snort.

Lauren felt a happy glow. She loved it when she and Twilight helped people together. 'I wonder who we'll help next,' she said to Twilight. A picture of Mrs Fontana came into her mind and she sighed. 'If only we could cure Mrs Fontana.'

'I wish we could,' Twilight agreed as they flew over the woods. 'But she said we couldn't help her.'

Lauren hesitated. The success of helping Hannah was still buzzing through her. 'I know she said that, but there must be something we can do,' she argued. 'Even if we can't take her illness away, maybe we can make her feel better somehow. We help everyone else.'

As she spoke, she spotted a glimpse of white at the edge of a clearing beneath them. 'What's that?'

'I think it's a unicorn!' Twilight snorted in surprise.

Lauren gasped. 'Quick! Let's go down and see it!'

Twilight cantered down through the trees. As they got closer, Lauren saw that it *was* a unicorn! A tall, very handsome unicorn with a long white mane and tail that swept to the floor and a glittering silver horn. A person was hurrying through the trees towards him.

'Twilight! It's Mrs Fontana!' Lauren hissed. The old lady moved with light, quick steps and even though Lauren and

Twilight were some way above her, Lauren could see the look of delight on the old lady's face. 'Do you . . . do you think it's Mrs Fontana's unicorn?' Lauren whispered to Twilight.

'I think it is,' Twilight said as the unicorn standing in the trees saw the old lady and whinnied.

Mrs Fontana broke into a run and the next second, she had thrown her arms around his neck and was hugging him and he was giving little whickers of joy.

Lauren felt Twilight hesitate and she understood. Seeing Mrs Fontana and her unicorn together, she had a feeling that they were intruding.

Mrs Fontana was talking to the

unicorn and he was nuzzling her shoulder. The unicorn bent his head as if saying something and Mrs Fontana nodded. To Lauren's amazement, she took hold of his mane and swung herself easily on to his back. As she sat there, Lauren didn't think she had ever seen anyone look quite so happy as the old lady did right then. The pain seemed to have vanished from her face.

'Mrs Fontana looks really well again,' she said. 'She must have got better.'

'She didn't need my magic after all,' Twilight said. He snorted suddenly. 'Look, Lauren!'

The unicorn plunged into the air with Mrs Fontana on his back. She held on to

his mane, her yellow shawl blowing out
behind her and her eyes sparkling. The
unicorn galloped up into the starry sky
and swooped away.

'They're flying!' Lauren gasped.

Mrs Fontana and her unicorn
disappeared into the darkness.

'They've gone,' Twilight said.

'I can't believe Mrs Fontana's unicorn came back,' Lauren said wonderingly. 'Do you think he's been in Arcadia all this time?'

'He must have been,' Twilight replied. 'I wonder if he's come back to the human world to live.'

Lauren remembered what Mrs Fontana had said. *One day we will meet again and never be parted.* She hugged Twilight. 'Oh, I bet that's what's happened. I'm so glad Mrs Fontana has got him back – and that she looks so well and happy.'

'It's brilliant!' Twilight agreed. He tossed his head. 'Should we go flying too, Lauren?'

'OK,' she grinned. 'Let's!'

CHAPTER

Nine

The next morning, Hannah got up to help Lauren with the ponies. They had arranged to go for a ride in the woods with Mel and Jessica that afternoon. 'You know, we could always go and change the book that I bought you for your birthday present,' Lauren said as they mucked out Magpie's stable. 'We could go this morning.'

'You wouldn't mind?' Hannah said.
'I mean, yesterday showed me how much
I like being with ponies but I don't think
I want to get into the whole showing
scene again so I'm not really going to
use that book.'

'Well, I don't mind you swapping it at
all,' Lauren said, glad her cousin was
being honest. 'I'd rather you had a book
you wanted.'

When they went inside she asked her
mum if they could go to the bookshop
and her mum agreed. However, when
they got there, just before lunchtime, the
bookshop had a 'closed' sign up.

'Oh dear,' Mrs Foster said. 'I hope the
shop's not shut because Mrs Fontana is ill.'

Lauren peered through the glass in the door. Surely Mrs Fontana couldn't be ill again. Not when she'd looked so well the night before. Suddenly her eyes caught a movement in the shop. It was Catherine, Mrs Fontana's niece. Seeing Lauren, Catherine came to the door.

'I'm sorry, we're not open today,' she said, opening the door. Her eyes were red as if she had been crying.

'Is everything OK?' Mrs Foster asked, looking at her in concern.

'Not really.' Catherine's voice caught on the words. 'My aunt passed away last night.'

Lauren stared. 'Mrs Fontana's dead?' she whispered.

Catherine nodded.

No, Lauren thought, her mind seeming to refuse to take it in. *It can't be true. Mrs Fontana can't be dead.*

'She died in her sleep last night. No one knows quite what time,' Catherine went on.

Lauren felt like a bucket of ice had just been dumped all over her. 'Last night!'

Catherine nodded.

But we saw her! Lauren only just bit the words back. Her mind whirled. Her mouth felt dry.

'I'm so sorry,' Mrs Foster said sympathetically to Catherine. 'We'll all miss her terribly. Our thoughts are with you and your family.'

'Thank you,' Catherine said, swallowing hard. She looked at Lauren and seemed to pull herself together. 'Lauren, this might not be the right time, but there was a letter on my aunt's desk this morning and it was addressed to you. If you can wait a moment I'll go inside and fetch it.'

'Of course we can,' Mrs Foster said.

Catherine hurried into the shop. A few moments later she returned with a thick cream envelope. On the front it said 'Lauren Foster'.

Lauren took it.

'I wonder what's inside it?' Hannah said uncertainly.

Lauren opened it up. There was a letter. She unfolded it:

Lauren,

My time is over – your time has come. Please don't feel sad. This is the way things have to be. Now is the time to open the box. Guard the secret well, my dear.

Much love, Mrs Fontana x

Lauren folded the letter quickly so that no one else would see it. 'It's just a short letter,' she whispered, forcing the words past a painful lump that was filling her throat. So it was true. Mrs Fontana was dead.

Beside her, her mum wiped her eyes. 'We'd better go home,' Mrs Foster said. 'I'll get you another book another time, Hannah.'

'Don't worry about it,' Hannah said quietly. 'It's not important.'

They got back into the car. Lauren felt as if she was moving automatically.

'Oh, poor Mrs Fontana,' Mrs Foster said. 'Poor Catherine.'

Hannah looked at Lauren. 'Are you OK?'

Lauren nodded but she'd never felt less OK in her life.

Mrs Foster looked at her pale face. 'Come on. Let's get home.'

All the way home, the thought echoed around Lauren's brain: *Mrs Fontana's dead*.

When they got back, she got out of the car in a daze.

Hannah glanced at her and seemed to decide that it was better to leave her on her own for a while. 'Shall I help you get lunch ready, Auntie Alice?'

'Yes please,' Mrs Foster replied. She hugged Lauren. 'Are you OK, honey?'

Lauren nodded. 'I think I'll just go and see Twilight,' she said numbly.

Mrs Foster nodded understandingly. 'I'll call you when it's lunchtime.'

Lauren walked down the path towards the field. Twilight was waiting by the gate. He whinnied and then snorted in concern when he saw her shocked face.

Lauren climbed over the fence. 'Oh, Twilight,' she whispered. 'Mrs Fontana's dead.'

Twilight stared at her.

'She died last night.' Lauren's brain swam in confusion. 'But I don't understand how she can have died then. We saw her!' Twilight stepped forward and began to nuzzle her face and hair.

Lauren wished desperately she could turn him into a unicorn so that he could talk to her. She suddenly remembered the letter she had shoved into her pocket. 'She left me this, Twilight.' She opened it and read it out to him in a halting voice. As she finished, she looked up. 'Now is the time to open the box,' she whispered. 'Should I go and get it?'

Twilight nodded and stamped a front hoof.

Lauren ran to the house and up the stairs. Luckily she didn't see her mum or Hannah. She picked up the chest and returned to the field.

'Here it is,' she said.

Twilight watched as Lauren turned the key in the lock. For a moment it seemed to catch but then it turned smoothly and

the clasp opened. Lauren lifted the lid.
Inside there was a thick purple book tied
with a silver ribbon, a dusty flat rock,
a scroll, a silver pendant shaped like a star
and five bottles of various sizes and colours.

There was some writing on the inside
of the lid that was old-fashioned and
swirly. She read it out:

'*This chest shall only be opened by a
Keeper of the Unicorns' Secrets. You,
like the other Keepers of Secrets around
the world, have been chosen to help the
secret unicorns and their friends. The book
will help you in this work. Share its
wisdom but do not try to do everything.
Remember that each unicorn and their*

friend must find their own way. Guard the book well and let no harm ever come to a unicorn from the words you say.'

Lauren stared at the writing. 'What? I'm what?'

She read it again and looked at Twilight. 'I'm a Keeper of the Unicorns' Secrets,' she said, hardly able to take it in. 'I've got to help other Unicorn Friends. Oh, Twilight, was Mrs Fontana a Keeper of the Unicorns' Secrets too?' Twilight nodded. His eyes were wide.

Lauren looked at the words. 'But how can I ever do what Mrs Fontana did?' she exclaimed. As she spoke, a picture of Mrs Fontana sprang into her mind – Mrs

Fontana with her blue eyes sparkling and a wise smile on her old face.

A sob tore through Lauren.

'Mrs Fontana. Oh, Mrs Fontana!' she said. Throwing her arms around Twilight's neck, she started to cry. Twilight nuzzled her hair over and over again.

Eventually the sobs subsided and Lauren's tears slowly dried up. Wiping her sleeve across her face, she sniffed. Her head was aching and her eyes felt sore.

Twilight breathed softly on her face, drying her remaining tears.

'I wish I could turn you into a unicorn,' she whispered, her heart aching. 'I'll turn you into a unicorn as soon as I can tonight.'

Twilight nodded.

'Lauren!' Mrs Foster called from the house.

Lauren took a deep breath. 'Coming,' she called. Giving Twilight a last hug, she walked slowly up the path.

CHAPTER
Ten

Mrs Foster looked at Lauren's face as she walked into the kitchen. 'Oh, Lauren,' she said softly. She hurried over and hugged her.

Not wanting to start crying again, Lauren swallowed hard.

'Mrs Fontana was old, honey,' her mum said. 'She wasn't well. I know it's dreadful but at least she won't be in pain any more. Come on, sit down.' She led her to the table. 'You don't have to eat anything if you don't want to, but try. It might make you feel a little better.'

Hannah looked at her sympathetically as she sat down. 'We don't have to go

out for that ride this afternoon. I guess you don't feel like it.'

Lauren hesitated. For the first time in her life she didn't feel like going out riding with her friends but she knew how much Hannah had been looking forward to it. And if she didn't go, she'd just hang around feeling unhappy. 'It's OK,' she said quietly. 'We can still go.'

Her mum squeezed her hand. 'It's probably good to do something to take your mind off things.'

Lauren nodded. They began to eat. It was macaroni cheese, one of her favourite meals, but she found she could only manage a few forkfuls and she was glad when the time came to clear away.

Afterwards, she and Hannah went down to the field and saddled up Magpie and Twilight. They were just putting their hats on when Jessica and Mel turned up. Lauren was dreading telling them the news but as soon as she saw them, she knew they had already heard. Their faces were worried.

'Hi, Lauren,' Mel said. 'Have . . . have you heard the news about Mrs Fontana?'

Lauren nodded. Mel and Jessica hadn't been friends with Mrs Fontana in the same way she had but they knew her and they knew how much Lauren liked her.

'Are you OK?' Jessica asked her.

'Yeah,' Lauren muttered.

Twilight nuzzled her arm.

'Do you still want to go for a ride?' Mel asked.

Lauren nodded and put her foot in the stirrup. 'Yes.' She swung herself on to Twilight's back as Hannah mounted Magpie and the four of them rode into the woods.

It was strange riding through the trees and remembering all the times she had met Mrs Fontana there, but there was something comforting about being with Twilight and the others. They rode to where the banks and hills were. Hannah had a great time on Magpie. He was fast but responsive and she soon had him cantering up and down the slopes. 'This is great!' she exclaimed.

She saw Lauren's face and looked guilty.

Lauren didn't want Hannah feeling bad for enjoying herself. After all, she'd never even met Mrs Fontana.

'It *is* fun, isn't it?' she said, forcing herself to smile. 'Come on, Twilight!' She cantered him after Magpie. 'Who wants a game of tag?'

'Me!' the others all cried.

They raced round, chasing each other on the ponies.

'We'll have to come here again when I next visit,' Hannah said when they finally began riding home.

'Yes, we could have a picnic if it was the summer,' Mel said.

'Maybe we could even ask if we could camp out here,' said Jess. 'And get Grace and Jo-Ann to come.'

'That sounds brilliant!' said Hannah. She began to plan with the others what they could do.

Lauren patted Twilight's neck and let them talk. The afternoon had been better than she had thought it would be, but now she was longing to turn him into a unicorn and for them to just be on their own.

After supper that night, Lauren helped Hannah pack her things so that they could spend as much time as possible with the ponies the next day before she had to go. Hannah smiled at Lauren as they finished and closed her case. 'Thanks. It's been brilliant being here, Lauren.'

'Will you ask your mum and dad if you can come again in the summer?' Lauren said.

'Definitely!' Hannah replied. 'Maybe I can stay for a whole week then. Oh, Lauren! Thanks for reminding me how much I like being with ponies. I'm never ever going to let myself forget again.'

'I won't let you!' Lauren said, smiling at her. 'I'm going to be emailing you photos of Twilight and Magpie all the time.'

'You'd better be!' Hannah said. She

yawned. 'I'm tired. It must be all the riding.'

They hugged each other and said goodnight. Lauren went to her room and waited for her parents to go to bed too. Luckily they liked to go to bed early because of having to be up to feed the animals on the farm in the morning. While Lauren waited, she looked through the chest. The book was very old and seemed to contain lots of information about the different types of unicorn magic and what it could be used for.

Lauren rubbed her head. It was fascinating but she couldn't take it in. She still couldn't quite believe that she was supposed to be one of the Keepers of the Unicorns' Secrets. How could she be? Surely she didn't know enough about unicorn magic.

As soon as the house was quiet, she pulled her jeans back on and crept outside.

Twilight was waiting for her. She said the spell and turned him into a unicorn.

'Oh, Lauren!' he snorted. 'I can't believe Mrs Fontana is dead.'

'I know,' Lauren said. 'And I'm supposed to be the next Keeper of the Unicorns' Secrets. But how, Twilight? I don't know enough.'

Twilight looked at her, his eyes deep and dark. 'Mrs Fontana wouldn't have chosen you if she didn't think you could do it, Lauren. And you've got the book and I'll help you.'

'I suppose,' Lauren said, feeling slightly comforted. 'What do you think we'll have to do?'

'Help unicorns and their friends, just like Mrs Fontana did.' Twilight looked thoughtful. 'I guess it means we have to start looking out for unicorns to help, instead of just helping your friends and the people that you meet with their problems.'

'So everything's going to change,' Lauren said.

'Things always do,' Twilight told her softly.

Lauren remembered the words of

Mrs Fontana's note. *This is the way it has to be*, she thought. She leaned her head against Twilight's warm neck. 'Do you think when Unicorn Friends die they get to go to Arcadia with their unicorns? Maybe that's where we saw Mrs Fontana going last night?'

'I'm not sure,' Twilight replied doubtfully.

'Maybe they are in Arcadia together,' Lauren said. She had an idea. 'I know. Why don't we use the rose quartz stones to look for them!'

Twilight could use his magic to see people wherever they were in the world. All he had to do was touch his horn to a rock of rose quartz.

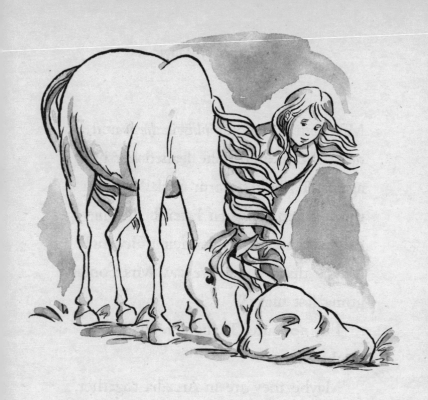

Lauren swung herself on to his back and they flew to the far end of the field where there were some rocks of rose quartz.

Lauren dismounted. Twilight looked at her and then touched his horn to one of the rocks. 'Mrs Fontana,' he said.

There was a faint purple flash and purple smoke covered the stone. As it cleared, Lauren could see that as usual the surface of the rock had begun to shine like a mirror. Her breath caught in her throat as she leaned forward. What were they going to see . . .?

Nothing.

The mirror shone but all that they could see was a swirling pinky-purple haze. There was no sign of Mrs Fontana.

'What's happened? Why's it not working?' Lauren frowned. They'd never tried to look at Arcadia before. 'Maybe we can't see into Arcadia.'

'Or maybe Mrs Fontana has gone

somewhere else where even unicorn magic can't see,' Twilight said.

They both stared at the rock. The pinky-purple haze moved. Lauren felt a sudden urge to touch the rose quartz. She reached out. As her fingers touched the shining surface, she gasped. A wave of warmth seemed to flood out from the stone. It wrapped around her, making her feel safe and loved.

Twilight snorted.

'Can you feel it too?' Lauren said in a trembling voice.

He nodded. 'It feels like . . . like Mrs Fontana's there.'

'Watching over us,' Lauren breathed. 'Caring about us.'

Twilight lifted his head. The rock stopped shining and Lauren felt the strength of the feeling fade but she was still left with a warm glow inside. She looked at Twilight.

'Even if we can't see her with your magic, Mrs Fontana's still there somewhere,' she said.

'And she's with her unicorn,' Twilight said. 'I felt it so strongly.'

An image of Mrs Fontana hugging her unicorn the night before filled Lauren's mind. She remembered the look of joy on the old lady's face, and the way she had looked so free from pain and worry. Lauren knew that she and Twilight would never see Mrs Fontana again but suddenly the thought didn't make her feel so sad. Mrs Fontana had been right. Things did change – it was the way life was – but change wasn't always bad. Mrs Fontana had gone but now she was with her unicorn again and this time they would never be parted.

And I'm a Keeper of the Unicorns' Secrets, Lauren thought. Excitement flickered through her at the thought. She and Twilight had so much to do – so many people to help, so many adventures to have. She remembered something Mrs Fontana had written: *your time has come*. 'It's our time now, Twilight,' she said softly.

Twilight nodded. 'We've got to help

other secret unicorns and their friends.'

Lauren looked up at the sky. The stars glittered brightly overhead. 'We'll do our best, Mrs Fontana. I promise,' she declared.

An echo of Mrs Fontana's wise voice seemed to float through her head. '*I know you will, my dears. You always do.*'

Lauren felt calm and happy. She put her arms around Twilight. Life changed. People changed. But there was one thing she knew for sure – she and Twilight would always love each other and be there for each other. That would never change.

She looked at her secret unicorn. 'I love you, Twilight.'

He pricked up his ears, bathed in
starlight. 'Always and ever?'

Lauren smiled. 'Forever,' she said.

Do you love magic, unicorns and fairies?

Join the sparkling

My Secret Unicorn

fan club today!

It's FREE!

You will receive
an exciting **online newsletter** 4 times a year,
packed full of fun, games, news and competitions.

How to join:

visit

mysecretunicorn.co.uk

and enter your details

or send your name, address, date of birth* and email address to:

linda.chapman@puffin.co.uk

Your details will be kept by Puffin only for the purpose of sending information regarding Linda Chapman and other relevant Puffin books. It will not be passed on to any third parties.

*If you are under 13, you must get permission from a parent or guardian

Notice to parent/guardian of children under 13 years old: please add the following to their email, including your name: 'I consent to my child/ward submitting his/her personal details as above'.